THE TALKING DRUMS

by Bill E. Neder

illustrated by
Elizabeth Wolfe

Harcourt

Orlando   Boston   Dallas   Chicago   San Diego

Visit *The Learning Site!*

www.harcourtschool.com

As the hot sun beat down on the African village, Jon and his grandfather left their hut and walked to the field. A cool wind blew in their faces.

Jon appeared to be thinking hard.

"What do you think about, young one?"
asked Grandfather. "Do you think of the
fruit we will pick today?"

Jon smiled. "No," he said. "I like the fruit
and its sweet juice, but that is not what I
am thinking about now."

Soon Jon and his grandfather had reached the fruit trees.

"Grandfather," he said, "Momma will have her baby soon. Maybe today. If we are out here in the field, we won't hear the news."

Grandfather patted the boy on the head.
"Don't worry, young one," he said. "If Momma
has the baby, we will know right away."

Jon looked startled. "How?" he asked.

"The talking drums will tell us," said
Grandfather.

5

"Talking drums?" asked Jon. "Are you making a joke, Grandfather?"

"No," Grandfather said. "Come, let's pick the fruit. Then I will tell you all about the talking drums."

Grandfather stepped up on his ladder.
He picked fruit and threw it down to Jon.
The boy put it in a sack.

The man and boy worked for a long time.
Pick, catch, pick, catch. The job created a
kind of rhythm. Pick, catch, pick, catch.

While the sun's heat swelled, so did Jon's sack of fruit!

Grandfather came down from the ladder. They each took a piece of fruit and bit into it. The sweet juice cooled them off.

"Now, please tell me what a talking drum is," Jon said.

Grandfather smiled. "I will do more than that. I will play one for you."

"Where is it?" asked Jon.

"You are sitting on it!" Grandfather laughed.

The startled boy jumped up. "This is only a tree log!" Jon cried.

"No," said Grandfather. "It is not like most logs. Look inside."

Jon said, "Grandfather, part of the inside is missing. The log is hollow!"

Grandfather explained. "Long ago, people first used tree logs for drums. They hollowed out the inside. Then they beat the log with short sticks. The sounds imitated the sounds of speech."

"I want to try!" Jon cried.

Grandfather found two short sticks. He sat by the log and hit it hard. Jon looked surprised.

"It spoke to me!" the boy cried.

"Yes," Grandfather laughed. "If you hit the drum the right way, you can make many sounds of speech."

Just then, Jon and his grandfather heard drums far away.

"They are talking drums!" Jon cried. "Let's hear what they are saying."

Jon and his grandfather listened quietly.
Then Jon let out a big yell.

"Momma had a baby boy!" he shouted.
"Hear the news, Grandfather! I have a new
baby brother! That suits me fine!"

The two flew back to the village as fast as they could. Many friends and family were there, waiting for them.

Two men sat with talking drums. They didn't need a conductor to lead them. They continued to play as people sang and danced to the rhythm.

Soon, everyone in the village appeared.
"A new baby boy!" they cried.
"A new baby brother!" Jon cried.
The whole village danced to the rhythm
of the talking drums into the night.